Four & Twenty
Dinosaurs

Four & Twenty Dinosaurs

by
Bernard Most

Voyager Books
Harcourt Brace & Company
San Diego   New York   London

To the High School of Art and Design in New York City

Requests for permission to make copies of any part of the work should be mailed to: Permissions Department, Harcourt Brace & Company, 6277 Sea Harbor Drive, Orlando, Florida 32887-6777.

First Voyager Books edition 1999
Hardcover edition published by HarperCollins, 1990
Voyager Books is a registered trademark of Harcourt Brace & Company.

Library of Congress Cataloging-in-Publication Data
Most, Bernard.
Four & twenty dinosaurs/by Bernard Most.
p. cm.
"Voyager Books."
Summary: Dinosaurs are substituted for the main characters in this illustrated collection of traditional nursery rhymes.
ISBN 0-15-201959-6 pb
1. Nursery rhymes. 2. Children's poetry. 3. Dinosaurs—Poetry.
[1. Nursery rhymes.] I. Title.
PZ8.3.M847Fo   1999
398.8—dc21   98-15869

F E D C B A

Printed in Singapore

The illustrations in this book were done in Pantone markers on hot press board.
Printed and bound by Tien Wah Press, Singapore
This book was printed on Arctic matte paper.
Production supervision by Stanley Redfern and Jane Van Gelder

Jack and Jill went up the hill,
To fetch a pail of water.
Jack fell down and broke his crown,
And Jill came tumbling after.
Said Jack to Jill, "That was no hill!
That was a Brontosaurus."

Peter Piper picked a peck of pickled peppers;
A peck of pickled peppers Peter Piper picked.
If Peter Piper picked a peck of pickled peppers,
Where's the peck of pickled peppers Peter Piper picked?

Rain on the green grass,
And rain on the tree,
Rain on the housetop,
But not on me.

Hark! Hark! The dogs do bark,
The dinosaurs are coming to town;
Some in rags and some in Jags,
And one in a velvet gown.

Pat-a-cake, pat-a-cake, baker's man,
Bake me a cake as fast as you can,
Pat it, and prick it, and mark it with a "B,"
Put it in the oven for Bactrosaurus and me.

Needles and pins,
Needles and pins,
When dinosaurs marry,
Their trouble begins.

London Bridge is falling down,
Falling down, falling down,
London Bridge is falling down,
My fair lady!

Build it up with iron and steel,
Iron and steel, iron and steel,
Build it up with iron and steel,
My fair lady!

Diddle, diddle, dumpling, my Iguanodon
Went to bed with his trousers on.
One shoe off, and one shoe on,
Diddle, diddle, dumpling, my Iguanodon.

"Bow-wow," say the dogs,
"Meow-meow," say the cats,
"Grunt-grunt," go the hogs,
And "squeak," go the rats.

"Caw-caw," say the crows,
"Quack-quack," say the ducks,
What did the dinosaurs say?
Nobody knows.

Little Miss Muffet sat on her tuffet,
Eating her curds and whey;
Along came a spider,
And sat down beside her.
Did it frighten Miss Muffet away?

Go to bed late,
Stay very small.
Go to bed early,
Grow very tall.

Higher than a house,
Higher than a tree,
Oh, whatever can that be?

Hush-a-bye, baby, in the treetop,
When the wind blows, the cradle will rock,
When the bough breaks, the cradle will fall,
Down will come baby, cradle and all.

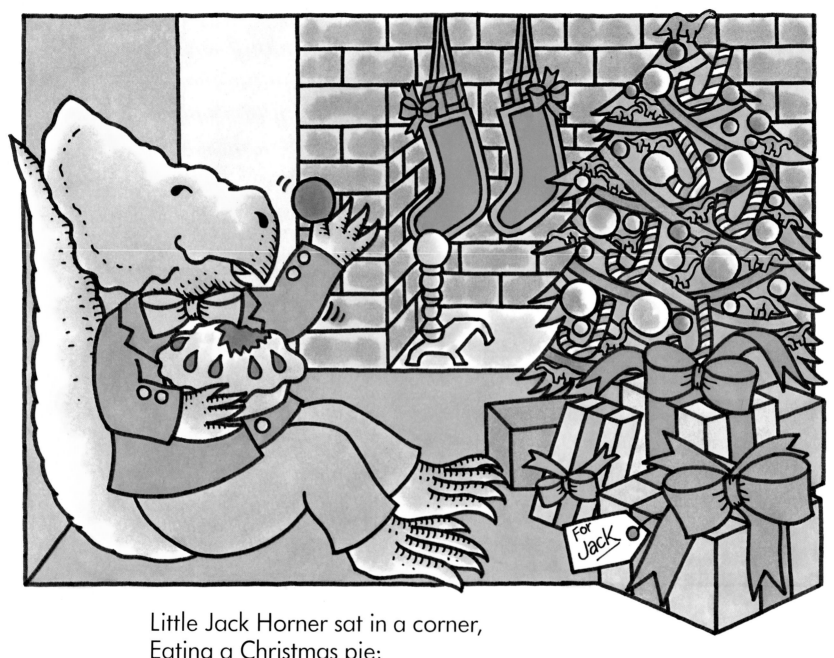

Little Jack Horner sat in a corner,
Eating a Christmas pie;
He put in his thumb, and pulled out a plum,
And said, "What a good Protoceratops am I!"

Here we go round the mulberry bush,
The mulberry bush, the mulberry bush,
Here we go round the mulberry bush,
On a cold and frosty morning.

One, two, three, four and five,
I caught an Allosaurus alive!
Six, seven, eight, nine and ten,
I let it go again.

Why did you let it go?
Because it bit my finger so!
Which finger did it bite?
The little finger on the right.

Old Mother Hubbard
Went to the cupboard,
To fetch her poor dog a bone.

But when she got there,
The cupboard was bare,
And so her poor dog had none.

Hey diddle, diddle,
Where's the cat and the fiddle?
Where's the cow that jumped over the moon?
Where's the little dog that laughed to see such sport?
Where's the dish that ran away with the spoon?

Cobbler, cobbler, mend my shoe,
Get it done by half past two.
Stitch it up, and stitch it down,
Then I'll give you half a crown.

Mary had a little Lambeosaurus,   It followed her to school one day,
With feet as white as snow.   Which was against the rule.
And everywhere that Mary went,   It made the children laugh and play,
The Lambeosaurus was sure to go.   To see a Lambeosaurus at school.

Sing a song of sixpence,
A pocketful of rye;
Four and twenty dinosaurs,
Baked in a pie.

When the pie was opened,
They all began to sing;
Was that not a dainty dish,
To set before the king?

Three little kittens,
They lost their mittens,
And they began to cry,
Oh mother dear, we sadly fear,
Our mittens we have lost.

What! lost your mittens,
You naughty kittens!
Then you shall have no pie.
Mee-ow, mee-ow, mee-ow,
No, you shall have no pie.

There was an old woman who lived in a shoe.
She had so many Triceratopses, she didn't know what to do.
She gave them some broth, without any bread,
She spanked them all soundly and sent them to bed.

The man in the moon,
Looked out of the moon,
Looked out of the moon and said:
"'Tis time for all Tyrannosauruses on earth,
To think about getting to bed!"